JAN MARK

MY FROG AND I

ILLUSTRATED BY

LESLEY HARKER

HAPPY CAT BOOKS

HAPPY CAT BOOKS

Published by Happy Cat Books Ltd.
Bradfield, Essex CO11 2UT, UK

This edition published 2005
1 3 5 7 9 10 8 6 4 2

Copyright © Jan Mark, 1997, 2005
Illustrations copyright © Lesley Harker, 1997, 2005

A CIP catalogue record for this book is available from the British Library

ISBN 1 903285 97 6

Printed in Poland

Chapter 1

I never had much luck until that Christmas when I was in year six. It wasn't even a very happy Christmas, not for me, because I had terrible toothache. It was because of the toothache that I got the good luck. Everyone else was watching a video of *Bugsy Malone* and I was curled up on the settee with a hot-water bottle under my face, and Mum found the very last cracker in the box and pulled it with me, to cheer me up. And he came out of the cracker.

He was a little metal frog. I thought
then that he was made of silver, but I don't
suppose he was really, not if he came out
of a cracker. I called him Bugsy because it
was a silly name for a frog.

Bugsy Frog lived under my ink well. Most people do not know what an ink well is, and neither did I the first time I saw one.

When we went up into 6RG our class was put in the old building. Most of Peel Green Middle is new, all flat and glassy, but up one end of the playground, near the road, is the old original school that was built in 1872, with a proper roof and a bell in a little tower. It is a listed building so it cannot be pulled down. The old school in *our* village was turned into a house when they closed it, and a swanky family live in it now. Even after *five years* they still don't talk to the neighbours, and they have three cars, but we all know that their conservatory is where the old outside toilets used to be. 'There's Lady Muck in the loo again,' we say loudly, as we go past.

It must have been nice in the old days, being able to go to school across the fields and not having to leave home until the last minute. From my bedroom window I can see the roof of the old school, and the footpath next to our house comes out just past it. I go along it every day to catch the bus into town, to the High School, but when I got Bugsy I was still at Peel Green. The journey was only ten minutes and we were always there on time. It was people who lived just across the road from school who were always late.

The worst thing was having to come out straight away at home time instead of hanging about with your mates. It still is. There aren't any service buses to our village and the one time I did miss the bus Dad had to come all the way to fetch me. At Peel Green we never had the chance to miss the bus. We were rounded up and herded on to it like bullocks going to market.

The old school at Peel Green was just one big room that went right up into the roof, but they got the builders in and cut it in half. One end was the staffroom and the other end was ours, but Mrs Gilchrist told us that once there were ninety children in it. They were all squashed into rows, on benches. It must have been like sitting in assembly all day.

The floors were made of wood and the furniture was old, too. We didn't have tables, we had double desks that sloped on top, and the seats were joined on to the desks. Each half of each desk had a flat place near the top of the slope with a long groove in it and a little round hole. A lot of the holes were empty, but some of them had white china pots in, like for paint water only much too small. My desk had one of those.

I said, 'What's this, Miss?'

Mrs Gilchrist said, 'That's an ink well.'

So then all the people who had ink wells took them out and looked at them until someone said, 'Miss, what are they for?'

'To put ink in,' Mrs Gilchrist said. 'Once upon a time ink was wet and you had to dip the pen into it and it made a terrible mess, I can tell you. And if you leaned on your elbow with the pen in your hand – like you're doing now Robert – instead of resting it in that groove, where it was meant to be, all the ink ran backwards down the pen and over your fingers. We all had blue fingers in those days and the really messy ones had blue arms as well.'

'What, like the Ancient Britons?' Leigh said, because we'd been doing the Ancient

Britons last year, all about how they dyed themselves blue before they went into battle.

Someone else said, 'Are you *that* old, Miss?'

Mrs Gilchrist said, 'The Ancient Britons wore woad, not ink, and it wasn't all that long ago, the days of dip pens. Every desk in every school had one of those ink wells and the ink was kept in a huge bottle. Somebody very good and very careful was chosen to be ink monitor and went round filling the ink wells. And very bad people filled up other people's ink wells with fluff and chalk and bits of blotting-paper.'

So then someone said, 'Miss, what's blotting-paper?'

Mrs Gilchrist said, 'Find out for homework. Your aged parents will be able to tell you. And remember, time doesn't stand still. One day your grandchildren will be asking you what chalk was.' Then she said, 'Now, stop fiddling with those ink wells or let me collect them up and put them away.'

But we liked our ink wells. No one else in the school had them, or desks with seats joined on, so we stopped fiddling and Mrs Gilchrist let us keep them. It was nice, taking them out sometimes and

putting them back, to see how they were exactly the right size for the holes in the desks. Some of us put water in them and had flowers.

My ink well was different. It wasn't

very deep and there was a gap between it and the bottom of the hole, just big enough to put something in. At first I kept sweets there, for emergency rations, but after I got Bugsy I put him in to see if he would fit, and he did. The gap was exactly the right size for Bugsy. I always took him to school after that and he sat under the ink well all day, right through the Easter term. No one else used that desk and no one else knew he was there. At first I used to take him home at night, but after a bit I left him there all the time except for half-term. He was my frog-in-the-hole, my secret good-luck frog. I didn't need good luck at home, but I always needed it at school.

At home if things go wrong you can

do something about it or, if you want something very badly, you can ask for it. If the answer's no, at least you know why. I didn't have a bike for ages because we couldn't afford it. It was the same with dancing lessons. Mum would have let me have dancing lessons if she could. Good luck wouldn't have helped. But at school it's different. If you don't get the part you want in a play, or you don't get chosen for a team, it's because there are so many people who want it too. They may not be better than you, they're just *there*, getting in the way of what you want, the same as you are getting in the way of what they want. Some really nice people would never get anything they wanted if they didn't have good luck. Crossing your fingers and

touching wood aren't enough. You have to have your own good luck. Bugsy was mine.

And then, when we came back after Easter, the ceiling fell in on class 7JF.

When we heard the news we all made jokes about it, saying whose head we hoped the ceiling had landed on, because 7JF were that sort of class. There's one in every school, it starts bad and gets worse. 7JF were the ones who were always made to stay back after assembly when there was trouble on the buses. And they never took any notice of us except to say snobby things and nick our lunches and that. You could imagine 7JF when they were in Reception, mini-skinheads with tiny DMs and the girls with sawn-off Cindy dolls and sharpened headbands to throw at people, like Oddjob's bowler hat in James Bond. Their teacher, Miss Flowers, was always yelling at them and sending them to stand outside the head teacher's room. 4CS were going the same way, but they were still small enough to push around.

Anyway, it turned out that 7JF weren't in their room when the ceiling fell in. It happened during the weekend when there was a storm and some of the flat roof blew off. So no one was killed, but after that

there were not enough rooms to go round
and it was like musical chairs. As soon as
a class went out of a room, another class
went into it, like, if 5EL were in the hall for
music, 7JF rushed into their room and had
French, and when the violin teacher came
she had to go in the staffroom next door to

us, and we could hear this horrible sawing, groaning noise going on all morning, like elephants with asthma. When we went out for games, 7JF came and had history in our room.

The first time it happened we didn't

know about 7JF. In the old building the windows were too high up to see in from outside, and it was only when we were coming back in after rounders that Damian Matthews looked through the glass half of

our door and said, 'Here, who's all those in our room?'

Mr Maldon said, 'Stop making a fuss, Damian.

You know perfectly well what's going on.' Teachers always say that. We are always meant to know what is going on, even when they have been muttering to each other outside the door and it's supposed to be a secret.

Well, when I saw that there were strange people in our room I thought, Bugsy! Because, of course, Bugsy Frog was under my ink well, and I knew what would have been going on. As soon as that other class saw the ink wells they would do just what we had done, they'd have taken them out and said, 'What's these?' and poked about in the holes. I went all cold, I was so worried about my frog.

And when I saw it was 7JF I felt cold again because there were some horrible people in 7JF, like Eddy Milford and Janine Amis and Stephen Walcott. Janine Amis was always nicking things – not secretly, she'd just come up to you and take them, like anything special you had, that you'd brought to school to show a friend. Janine Amis would grab it and dance round the

playground, holding it in the air so you'd have to jump up and down to try and get it. Then she'd chuck it away saying, 'Who wants this old rubbish?' so you'd feel ashamed of it afterwards. Stephen Walcott didn't steal things, he broke them. Everything Stephen touched came to pieces, pens and books and sandwiches and that. It was a whole chair, once. Bugsy would be squashed flat if Walcott had got him.

We went into the classroom as 7JF came crashing out, and I ran straight to my desk and took out the ink well. Bugsy Frog was not there, but where he should have been was a little piece of paper, folded up small. It was a note.

IF YOU WANT TO SEE YOUR FRIEND AGAIN LEAVE SOME CHEWING-GUM IN THE HOLE. TRY ANY TRICKS AND THE FROG GETS IT.

It wasn't signed. Kidnappers never give away their names.

Chapter 2

I thought about 7JF all the way home, wondering which one of them was the frognapper and thinking what a horrible lot they were to steal my frog. Then I thought, well, only *one* of them stole him, and then I thought, he hasn't really been stolen. If the frognapper was a *really* horrible person they would have just taken him, so that ruled out Janine Amis. If Janine had taken him she'd want me to know about it. She'd have walked past me and held him under my nose. And then she'd have thrown him away.

So I thought that really the ransom note was quite like a sort of joke, and I was glad I hadn't made a fuss and tattled to Mrs Gilchrist.

Next day in assembly I looked round at 7JF who were behind us. I looked hard and hoped the frognapper would feel guilty, but then I realised that the frognapper didn't know whose frog it was. If we'd had trays under the desks to keep our books in, like the rest of the school, the frognapper would have known my name, or they could have looked, if they'd wanted to, but we didn't. We kept our books in lockers (well they were called lockers, but none of them had keys).

Afterwards I said to Mrs Gilchrist,
'When are 7JF in our room again, Miss?'

'Next time you have games or PE, I
suppose,' she said. 'And, Jane, don't think
I didn't notice you fidgeting about in
assembly. Why do you want to know?'

I could have told her about Bugsy then,

but I knew she would only say, 'Why didn't you report this yesterday?' and then, 'It is very silly to leave valuable things lying about. We're always telling you that.' Anyway, if she *had* known there would have been a lot of fuss – and I remembered the note. Bugsy would have got it if I'd tattled.

So I just said, 'Yes, Miss.' Anyway Bugsy was only valuable to *me*. No one was going to turn the school upside down to find a tin frog only fifteen millimetres long. But if something is special it doesn't have to be worth money. I had a bit of brick once, that we picked up on the beach. The sea had worn it smooth and round and it was full of holes. I thought it was a fossilised sponge and I went on calling it that even after Dad told me what it really was. It got lost when we moved and I was so upset. It would be much worse if I lost Bugsy for ever.

We had PE the day after, Friday, and I had some chewing-gum ready. I'd been practising. I had to fold it in three to get it into the ink well hole and it wouldn't lie flat. It kept pushing the ink well out of the hole, like a spring. So then I took it out of its wrapper and squashed it and folded it up in the silver paper, and then I thought, I'll get you back for napping my frog, so I chewed it up and *then* wrapped it in the silver paper.

We went out for PE, walking in a line like Mrs Gilchrist always made us, and I saw 7JF coming the other way in a stampede because no one could make them stay in line except Mr Maldon, and I went all cold again. They *were* horrible, they were all horrible. The frognapper would be mad when they found the chewing-gum and Bugsy *would* get it. I couldn't concentrate in PE and I fell off the bars and banged my knee, all because my good-luck Bugsy Frog had been taken. Then I remembered how on Wednesday, in rounders, I got a splinter off the manky old bat and I thought, that must have been the *exact* moment when Bugsy was frognapped and I lost my good luck.

Mr Maldon let me sit out after I banged my knee so I got changed first and I was first in line to go back to our room in the old building. But I was limping because of my poorly knee so I was the last one in after all, and 7JF were out and walloping around all over the playground.

I looked round the classroom. You'd never think that they'd had a teacher in there with them. There were scribbles on the board and crisp packets and sweet wrappers all over the floor and bits of file paper with footprints on. There was a biscuit in Mrs Gilchrist's vase of flowers, you could see it through the glass, all pale and swollen up. Even though the desks had iron frames they were pushed out of place, and someone had been stomping on chalk at the back. What hadn't been stomped on was stuck in the ink wells,

just like Mrs Gilchrist had told us.

There was nothing stuck in my ink well when I went to look, but underneath was another piece of paper and wrapped in the paper was Bugsy Frog. I couldn't believe it! Then I saw some writing on the paper. It said:

THAT WAS A DIRTY TRICK BUT I ALWAYS KEEP MY WORD.

I thought, there is one person in 7JF who is not completely horrible, but I was not taking any more risks and I decided that after this I would always keep Bugsy Frog in my pocket. But on Monday, when we had PE, I got a nice fresh piece of chewing-gum (unchewed) and put it under the ink well with another note that said:

Sorry. You are all
right really.

When we came back afterwards I took

out the ink well and there was a Smartie and my note with something written on the back:

WHAT DO YOU MEAN, ALL RIGHT? I AM TOTALLY SPLENDITIOUS.

That week in games I got three rounders and I caught Suzannah Morley out, all because Bugsy Frog had come back to me. I put an Opal Fruit under the ink well that day and when I came back there was another note:

YOU ARE ALL RIGHT TOO. CAN I HAVE ANOTHER LOOK AT YOUR FROG?

So, on Friday, I put Bugsy back under the ink well and wrote a tiny letter on the back of a till roll receipt:

Dear Splenditious,
This is Bugsy Frog. He is my good luck.
Please do not take him away again.

It is difficult to write small but I left a little space to sign my name and then I thought, No I won't. That would spoil things. I don't know who Splenditious is and they don't know who *I* am.

Bugsy was still there when I came in again, wrapped up in an instant coffee token, *10p off*. There was a message, written round the edge of the token so that the end met the beginning and I took ages to work out where it started.

I THOUGHT BUGSY MUST BE LUCKY. WHEN I HAD HIM I GOT ALL MY FRENCH RIGHT AND MY GRAN TOOK ME TO A CONCERT. HE IS ACE.

Chapter 3

After that I stopped looking at 7JF in case someone in 7JF saw me looking and we recognised each other. I didn't want to know who Splenditious was and I didn't think they wanted to know who I was, and, anyway, I couldn't imagine who they were. I couldn't even begin to guess. People in 7JF didn't go to concerts with their grannies. It might have been a Heavy Metal concert, but your granny wouldn't take you to that. I went through the whole lot, all thirty of them, hoping it wasn't this person or that person. I ended up hoping it wasn't any of them but I knew that it must be, and I always left Bugsy under the ink well when we had PE or games or music, with a note, and there was always a note for me afterwards.

One day it said:

WARNING!!!!! DO NOT LEAVE BUGSY ON FRIDAY. I AM GOING TO THE DENTIST AND HE MIGHT FALL INTO THE WRONG HANDS.

I was really grateful that Splenditious had thought of that, but I was always a bit worried anyway, in case they got ill suddenly and couldn't let me know that Bugsy was in danger. I wrote that on a bit of box lid. Splenditious wrote back on the other side:

NEVER FEAR. I AM AN EXTREMELY HEALTHY
PERSON AND I WOULD HAVE TO BE DEAD
TO MISS A DATE WITH BUGSY.

But just before half term there was a
message that said:

I DON'T FEEL VERY WELL TODAY. BETTER
KEEP BUGSY OUT OF SCHOOL UNTIL I MAKE
CONTACT AGAIN.

I realised then that Splenditious must
know how horrible the rest of 7JF were.
Then I wondered if Splenditious had to
pretend to be horrible just so as not to get
picked on, like now, at the High School,

where you have to pretend to be stupid and lazy or you get called a swot and no one wants to be seen talking to you. And I did wonder if all of 7JF were like that, all pretending to be horrible and not daring to stop because they were afraid of the others. Perhaps they were all ever so nice underneath and would not harm Bugsy, but I was not going to risk trying to find out. Because probably they were not like that at all.

Then one day Splenditious must have slipped into the old building before school started, because when I went to put a Mint Imperial under the ink well I found a message there already. It said:

PLEASE MAY I BORROW BUGSY FOR THE

WEEKEND? I WILL TAKE GREAT CARE OF HIM, ONLY, I NEED SOME GOOD LUCK VERY BADLY.

I wrote:

Of course. Good luck from me, too.

and squashed it into the hole with Bugsy. There was no room for the Mint Imperial so I ate it.

Bugsy came back on Monday with good news:

THIS FROG IS THE BEST. SUPER-FROG! I HAD A MUSIC TEST. I PASSED. I AM IN THE YOUTH ORCHESTRA.

So now I knew one more thing about Splenditious. Splenditious was musical – but not the sort of music we did at school. You never saw anyone in 7JF with a musical instrument. Blunt instrument, more like. I remembered the concert, and how surprised I had been to think that Splenditious went to things like that. Then I thought, this is the kind of news that gets read out in assembly. Now I shall know who Splenditious really is, and all that week I waited to hear about it, but nothing was ever said. Nobody mentioned the youth orchestra.

First I wondered if Splenditious had made it all up, but I was sure they wouldn't do that, and I guessed that it was a secret, our secret; me and Splenditious and Bugsy. It was an odd thing to keep a secret, almost as if it was something to be ashamed of, but then I remembered that Splenditious was in 7JF. 7JF probably thought that being in an orchestra *was* something to be ashamed of and Splenditious would get beaten up.

Anyway, when I found the note I wrote back:

Congratulations. What do you play?

CLARINET. DO YOU PLAY ANYTHING?

Only rounders.

But there was another thing that I knew
about Splenditious. 7JF were the year above
us. They were the top year. At the end of
term Splenditious would be leaving.

Chapter 4

One day I looked at the calendar. There were only two weeks of term left and there was sports day coming up and the play and the fund-raising fête. Lessons were going to be all over the place and the builders still hadn't put the roof back on 7JF completely. In fact, they were taking some more roof off the next room as well, so *everyone* was going to be all over the place. We never knew when we were going to be called out of our room for practices and rehearsals, and we never knew who was going to be in it when we were out.

What I really wanted to do was to get properly in touch with Splenditious, leave a note that said something like, *We cannot go on meeting like this. Tell me who you are.* Well, I didn't really want to do that. We were only friends because we didn't know each other, like on the Internet, only we weren't meeting in cyberspace, we were meeting in that hole under the ink well; frogspace. But suddenly it looked as if we wouldn't even be meeting there, any more. Even though our class didn't like sharing with 7JF, they did sort of belong in our room now; it was the other classes who were the trespassers.

In the end I wrote a desperate note to Splenditious:

We are running out of time. I want you to have Bugsy Frog when you leave. I love him very much and I shall miss him, but if you have him I shall know that we are still friends for always.

After I'd written it I hoped and hoped that Splenditious would say, No, I couldn't possibly … and I nearly ran back to take the note out of the hole, but it was too late. 7JF had already gone in and the door was shut.

*   *   *

We were practising for sports day. I was
third in the relay team and I dropped
the baton when Suzannah passed it to
me. It wasn't Bugsy's fault, I just couldn't
concentrate, thinking about Splenditious

leaving and taking Bugsy with them. I thought, what shall I do for good luck when Bugsy's gone? and I didn't even see Suzannah coming. Mrs Gilchrist said, 'Jane, if you can't pay attention you'd better give up your place to someone who can,' and the rest of the team were booing and hooting.

All the same, I knew I'd be hurt if Splenditious said, No, thanks. Once, when I was little, I offered to lend someone my woolly horse to borrow for the night and they said, 'No, why?' and I said, 'You can take it to bed with you,' and they just said, 'I don't want it.' They weren't being mean or anything, they just didn't want it, and said so. I couldn't believe that someone wouldn't want my woolly horse, because I loved it so much. We were never really friends after that, and these days when someone offers me something, I always say, Yes, please, even if I don't want it.

So I was relieved when Splenditious wrote back:

ARE YOU SURE? THAT WOULD BE INCREDIBLE. WITH BUGSY BY MY SIDE I MIGHT BECOME A WORLD-FAMOUS SOLOIST. I LIVE NEAR SCHOOL SO I COULD COME EARLY BEFORE ASSEMBLY TO FETCH HIM.

There was no going back now. I wrote:

I will keep Bugsy until the day before we break up. You can collect him on the last morning.

It was a good thing that we thought of this because I was right about the lessons. One day we came back from a play rehearsal and we found 4CS in our room and all the ink wells were out of their holes because Miss Styles was useless and couldn't control 4CS even though they

were so little. You could see that 4CS were going to be just like 7JF in two years time; they were getting in shape already.

Suppose I'd left Bugsy Frog under the ink well and one of 4CS had got him?

For those last few days of term I kept Bugsy with me *every minute* because I was going to part with him for ever, and when I thought about that I was sad because I was going to lose Splenditious too. But on the day before we broke up I wrapped Bugsy in tissue paper and put him under the ink well with my last ever note. I wrote:

Goodbye Splenditious. I won't say good luck because I am giving you all my luck with Bugsy. Take care of him.

And then I went outside and got on the bus very quickly with a lot of the other girls, so I wouldn't have a chance to change my mind.

Next morning I woke up early which I never do most mornings. I sleep right through the alarm clock and Mum has to yell up the stairs. It was six o'clock. I lay in bed and thought, this is the day that Bugsy goes, and I thought of Bugsy there in the old building, spending his last hours under the ink well.

Then I realised why I had woken up. If I got up now I could get a lift in with Dad instead of waiting for the school bus, and I could lie in wait for Splenditious. I could even get in first and leave a different note, saying that I wanted to keep Bugsy after all, but then I wondered how Splenditious would feel when they found the note and no Bugsy, and I wondered how I would feel, too, so I didn't get up, I just stayed there and listened to Dad going out and banging the car door and driving away. Then I got up like usual, and caught the bus with the others and when I got to school I went to our room and took out the ink well. Bugsy had gone.

Bugsy had gone for ever. But in his place was the tissue paper wrapped round something flat. I thought it was a pound coin at first, but it was a piece of glass, the colour of amber. And there was a note, of course. The last note:

I POKED THIS OUT OF THE STAINED
GLASS WINDOW IN OUR BACK DOOR. IT'S
NOT VALUABLE OR EVEN LUCKY, BUT THE
WORLD LOOKS WONDERFUL THROUGH IT.
YOU ARE THE BEST FRIEND EVER. GOODBYE
FROM SPLENDITIOUS AND BUGSY.

I was so sad then, I thought I would
never stop. I wanted to run out of the room

and find class 7JF and shout 'Splenditious!'
just so I'd know at least who it was. But I
didn't. That would have spoiled everything.

Even being sad was part of it.

And Splenditious was right about the piece of glass. When I put it to my eye, everything looked like sunshine.

Chapter 5

When we came back in September, *we* were 7JF and we weren't in the old building any more. The roof had been put back on and we were over in the new part, next to the kitchen, so at least we were always first in the hall at lunch-time.

No ink wells any more, either. We missed our ink wells and hated the thought of Mrs Gilchrist's new class using them. I wondered who had my old desk and whether they kept anything under the ink well. We had ordinary tables now, with trays underneath to keep our books in. I never left my piece of yellow glass lying around. It lived in my pencil-case in a little special bag I made out of some velvet Mum gave me. I never showed it to anyone, and when I wanted to look through it I went off somewhere private and thought about Bugsy and Splenditious. I wondered what Splenditious was doing now, and how they were getting on with the clarinet. But I was sure they must be doing well because of Bugsy.

We had a good time being 7JF. We were in the top year now, along with 7LR and 7TM, only, we never thought much of them. There was no one to push us around. Miss Flowers must have enjoyed having us after the other lot. She got all nice and smiley again like she used to be, and she stopped being away so much with all the sore throats she got from yelling.

And even though I didn't have Bugsy any more I didn't lose my good luck after all. It didn't go away with him. So I didn't get anything else instead.

People had all sorts of mascots. During tests the room looked like a zoo, with hairy creatures sitting on the desks. But my desk was empty. There could never be another Bugsy.

And the end of the year came round again, and it was our turn to leave, and some of us knew we wouldn't see each other again because we were going to different schools in the city; the Boys' High and the Girls' High and the Roman Catholic one, St Augustine's. There were some people I was pleased about not seeing again, and some I was sorry about, but not *that* sorry. I knew I would never be as sorry again as I was about Bugsy and Splenditious.

The Girls' High School was really big and I didn't know anybody there except the girls who'd come up with me from Peel Green, and some people who'd gone there before us, but I never even wondered if one of them was Splenditious. They all looked so grown-up, and Splenditious would always be twelve, sort of, and, of course, I'd never known if Splenditious was a girl or a boy. Sometimes I'd be sure it was a boy, which was one of the reasons I'd never told anyone else about Splenditious and Bugsy and the notes. But then I'd think of all the boys in 7JF and be sure that Splenditious was a girl – till I remembered Janine Amis. In the end I stopped trying to guess. Splenditious was Splenditious.

Janine Amis had gone to St Augustine's.

On the first morning at the High we were met off the bus by a teacher who called out our names and sent us off with big girls. They showed us to our classrooms and told us where the cloakrooms were. There were seven in our class who'd come up with me from Peel Green and when we sat down at our

tables I was stuck next to a girl who'd been in 7LR and I hardly knew her. Her name was Teresa Milford and I'd never wanted to know her. Her brother was Eddy Milford who'd been in 7JF the year before with Janine Amis and Stephen Walcott. And Splenditious.

We hadn't even sat together on the bus, so we just looked at each other and got out our pencil-cases and wrote our names on our new books and files while the teacher told us rules. Teresa Milford opened her pencil-case. She took out a ruler. She took out a pen. She took out a little metal frog and sat him on the table. I looked at that frog. I couldn't believe it. Teresa saw me looking.

'That's Bugsy,' she said. 'He's for good luck.'

I couldn't believe it. I couldn't believe I was seeing Bugsy again and I couldn't believe that Splenditious would have given him away. I said, 'Can I look?' and picked him up before she could say no. 'Where did you get him?'

She said, 'He isn't mine. My brother lent him to me just for today. Bugsy's special.

He says his best friend gave him Bugsy, but I was scared about starting here and *my* best friend's gone to St Augustine's, so he said I could have him with me just this once.' Then she looked scared again because I was still *gripping* Bugsy and she said, 'Oh, give him back. Eddy'll go mad if I lose him.'

I must have looked loopy sitting there with my mouth open. I was thinking, Eddy? Your brother? *Your brother with Bugsy?* I was remembering Eddy Milford. He was a big, loud yobbo and of all the people that I hated in 7JF he was the one I hated most. He broke my watch once. He ran into me in the playground while I was holding it to change the date, and then put his big boot on it. He got wrong with

Miss Flowers and Mr Maldon for that, but he swore it was an accident and I couldn't prove it wasn't.

I got him back, though, that time. I upset my orange juice in his sports bag at break. Well I didn't *upset* it, I bit the corner off the carton and put it inside, upside down. He must have known I did it. He probably hated me, too.

And I was really pleased when he got

thrown out of the choir for mucking about.
He said the songs were rubbish. I remember
him walking out of the door. Miss Flowers
said, 'That's your last warning Edmund.
Don't come back.' And he said, 'Good. I
shan't have to sing this rubbish any more.'
I thought the songs were lovely, then, but
he didn't. Nor do I, now.

I said to Teresa, 'Where's your brother now, then?' and I was thinking, Eddy Milford playing the clarinet? He wasn't even in the Recorder Club.

Teresa said, 'He was at the Boys' High, but he's got a music scholarship to a school in London. He wants to be a musician. He says Bugsy got him the scholarship. *Please* give him back. Eddy'll need him. He starts his new school next week.'

I thought of all the things I could do. I could refuse to give Bugsy back. I could whip out my piece of yellow glass and say, That came out of your back door, didn't it? I could say, Tell your brother …

But I didn't say any of those things. I gave Bugsy back to Teresa and said, 'He must be a very special frog. Did you hear what that teacher was saying? We have to be in pairs when we go to the canteen for lunch. Have you got anyone to go in a pair with?'

And she said, 'No.'

And I said, 'You come in with me.'

Also by Jan Mark

THE DEAD LETTER BOX

Louie's best friend, Glenda, is moving away and they need a good way to keep in touch. In an old film that Louie once saw, spies left letters for each other in a dead letter box – a secret place in a hollow tree. Well, the girls didn't have a suitable tree but Louie had another great idea…

"…a grand readaloud and a terrific enrichment to
library lessons"
School Librarian

"How Louie makes a new friend is told sympathetically and realistically by Jan Mark whose instinct for the feelings and thoughts of young children is always on target"
Books for Keeps

BIOGRAPHICAL NOTE

Jan Mark grew up in Kent and attended Canterbury College of Art. She worked as a secondary-school teacher before starting to write full time. Her first book, *Thunder and Lightnings*, was published in 1976.

As well as writing she visits schools and colleges to talk about writing and to run workshops. Her books and stories are usually set in places where she has lived and worked, such as Norfolk, where *My Frog and I* takes place, Gravesend, where she used to teach, and Oxford, where she now lives.

Other titles by Jan Mark

Long Lost	*Macmillan (Shock Shop)*
The Snow Maze	*Walker*
Taking the Cat's Way Home	*Walker*
Lady Long-legs	*Walker*

Slightly older...

The Lady With Iron Bones	*Walker*
Eyes Wide Open	*A & C Black*